For Fred Bear, with love xxx

A TEMPLAR BOOK

First published in hardback and softback the UK in 2014 by
Templar Publishing, an imprint of The Templar Company Limited,
Deepdene Lodge, Deepdene Avenue,
Dorking, Surrey, RH5 4AT, UK
www.templarco.co.uk

ISBN 978-1-78370-054-7 (hardback)
ISBN 978-1-78370-100-1 (softback)

Printed in China

Bear Hug

Katharine McEwen

templar publishing

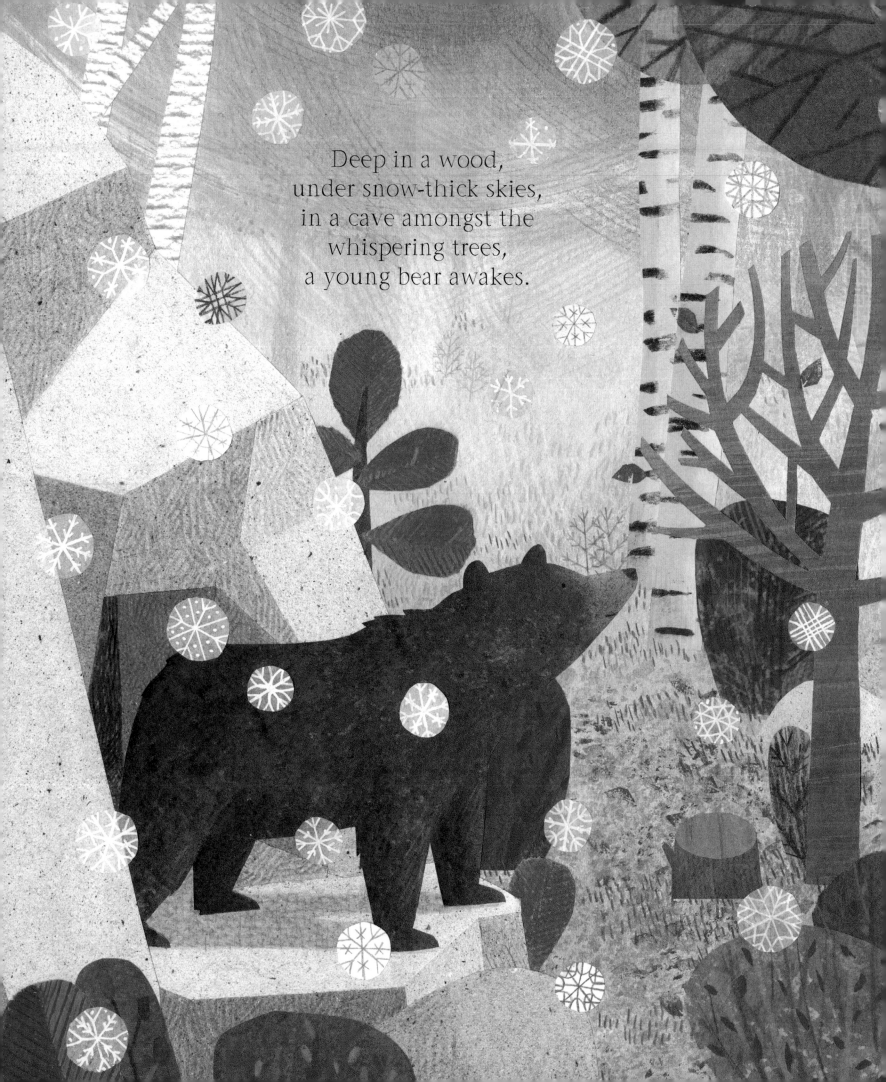

Deep in a wood,
under snow-thick skies,
in a cave amongst the
whispering trees,
a young bear awakes.

Sniffing the wintry air,
he knows he must get ready
for the cold nights ahead.

So just like Papa showed him,
he gathers leaves and bundles of bracken
to make a warm winter bed.

And just like Mama showed him,
he dives into the shivery river
to catch fat, silvery fish.

Then, one day, a friendly face
appears across the water –
another bear, young like him.

Amongst the frosty moss and riverside rocks,
the two hungry bears gather together
to share their catch.

As the days get colder, they fill their bellies
with juicy berries, feasting
until they're full.

When the icy skies darken
and the snowflakes twirl and tumble,
the two bears lollopy-lumber back to the cave.

And there, against the shudder-cold night,
on a soft bracken bed, the bears stay snug
in a big bear hug.

All winter long, the bears soundly sleep.

The woods rest too,
under a deep, downy
blanket of snow.

Then, early one morning,
the bears are awoken by a bold
and beautiful sound.

They sniff the air.
It is warm and fresh, and
the woodland is brimming
with birdsong.

Blinking in the sunshine,
they know at last
spring has arrived.

And before long there is another arrival,
soft as thistledown
and lively as a sunbeam...

their little bear cub!

As the days grow longer and the nights get shorter, life fills the forest.

Bees buzz busily in honey-filled hives.

Fat, silvery fish swim in the river.

And when the nights grow longer
and the days get shorter,

the cub gathers leaves,
just like Papa shows him.

And when the air gets colder
and frost nips at his nose,
the cub catches fish in the shivery river,
just like Mama shows him.

As they did, he learns
everything he needs to one day
adventure on his own.

But now,
as the snows come
and the icy winds return,

it is time to settle down
for the long winter sleep.

Cosy in the cave,
safe until the spring,
they slumber – a little bear family,
warm and snug in a big bear hug.